THIS CANDLEWICK BOOK BELONGS TO:

_____

_____

_____

_____

Homage to Cosmo

First U.S. paperback edition 1996

The Library of Congress has cataloged the hardcover edition as follows:
Ashforth, Camilla.
Calamity / Camilla Ashforth.— 1st U.S. ed.
Summary: Toy bear and rabbit James and Horatio accept a
disaster-prone donkey's challenge to race.
ISBN 1-56402-252-8 (hardcover)
[1. Toys—Fiction.   2. Racing—Fiction.] I. Title.
PZ7.A823Cal   1993
[E]—dc20   92-54956
ISBN 1-56402-568-3 (paperback)

2 4 6 8 10 9 7 5 3 1

Printed in Hong Kong

The pictures in this book were done in watercolor.

Candlewick Press
2067 Massachusetts Avenue
Cambridge, Massachusetts 02140

CALAMITY

Camilla Ashforth

CANDLEWICK PRESS
CAMBRIDGE, MASSACHUSETTS

James and Horatio were
building a tower.
"One, two, three," said James
as he balanced the blocks.
"Seven, four," added Horatio.

"HEE-HAW!"

BUMP!

Something crashed into the Useful
Box and sent everything flying.

"What was that?" asked Horatio.
"It's a calamity," said James,
looking at the mess.
"What were you doing, Calamity?"
asked Horatio.
"Racing," Calamity said. "And I won."

"Can I race?" asked Horatio.
"Find yourself a jockey," Calamity said.
"Here's mine." She turned around.
But that's a bobbin, thought James.
He started to clean up.

Horatio looked for a jockey.
I like this one, he thought.
It was James's clock.
"Are you ready?" asked Calamity.
They waited a moment.

"One, two, three, go!" Calamity called. She hurtled around the Useful Box. Twice.

Horatio tried to move his jockey.

He pushed it

and pulled it.

Then he rolled
it over.

His jockey would not budge.

Calamity screeched to a halt.

"Hee-haw! I won!" she bellowed.

"Let's race again."

James turned around.

He picked up Horatio's jockey.

"That's my clock," said James, and he put it in his Useful Box.

Horatio looked for another jockey.

"One, two, three, go!" Calamity called.
She galloped very fast.
Backward and forward.

Horatio looked around.
I'll go this way instead, he thought,
and he set off with his new jockey.

"Hee-haw! Won again!" cried
Calamity, stopping suddenly.
Horatio looked puzzled.
"One more race," Calamity said.
"I'm good at this."

"James," whispered Horatio, "will
you help me win this time?"

"What you need is a race track," said James. "I'll make you one."

"That block is the start," he said.

"And this string is the finish line.
Ready, set, go!"

Calamity thundered off.
She was going the wrong way.

Horatio headed for the finish line
as fast as he could.

Calamity turned in a circle and
headed back toward James.

"Stop!" James cried.

As Horatio crossed the line, Calamity
collided with the Useful Box.
CRASH!

"That was a good race. Who won?"
asked Calamity.
"I think you both did," James said,
and squeezed Horatio tight.

Camilla Ashforth's stories about James and Horatio, introduced to readers in her first book, *Horatio's Bed*, were inspired by the stuffed animals of her childhood. She based the character of Calamity on her son. "When he learned to run," she says, "he ran like a blown leaf across the yard and would 'win' just by stopping. Calamity is like him. She's not aggressively competitive—she just loves to run."

Also by Camilla Ashforth:
Horatio's Bed
Monkey Tricks
Humphrey Thud